THREE SKETCHES
FROM A HUNTER'S ALBUM

Ivan Turgenev

Three Sketches
from a Hunter's Album

TRANSLATED BY RICHARD FREEBORN

PENGUIN BOOKS

PENGUIN BOOKS
Published by the Penguin Group
Penguin Books USA Inc., 375 Hudson Street,
New York, New York 10014, U.S.A.
Penguin Books Ltd, 27 Wrights Lane,
London W8 5TZ, England
Penguin Books Australia Ltd, Ringwood,
Victoria, Australia
Penguin Books Canada Ltd, 10 Alcorn Avenue,
Toronto, Ontario, Canada M4V 3B2
Penguin Books (N.Z.) Ltd, 182–190 Wairau Road,
Auckland 10, New Zealand

Penguin Books Ltd, Registered Offices:
Harmondsworth, Middlesex, England

Published in Penguin Books 1995

These selections are from Richard Freeborn's translation of *Sketches from a Hunter's Album*, The Complete Edition, published by Penguin Books.

ISBN 0 14 60.0184 2

Printed in the United States of America

Contents

THREE SKETCHES
FROM A HUNTER'S ALBUM

Loner

One evening I was by myself in my racing droshky after
going hunting. There were still some half-dozen miles before I got home. My good trotting mare went happily
along the dusty road, occasionally giving snorts and
twitching her ears; my tired dog, as though literally tied
there, never for a moment fell back behind the rear
wheels. A thunderstorm was threatening. Straight ahead
an enormous lilac cloud rose slowly beyond the forest and
long grey lengths of cloud hung above me and stretched
towards me. The willows rustled and murmured in alarm.
The muggy heat was suddenly replaced by moist cool air
and the shadows thickened. I struck the horse with a rein,
descended into a gully, made my way across a dry stream
completely overgrown with willow bushes, went uphill
and drove into the forest. The road wound its way ahead
of me between thick clumps of nut, already immersed in
darkness, and my progress was difficult. The droshky
jumped about as the wheels struck the hard roots of
centuries-old oaks and limes which crisscrossed the deep
ruts made by cartwheels, and my horse began to stumble.
A strong wind suddenly began roaring on high, the trees
began thrashing about, huge raindrops started pounding
sharply on the leaves and splashing over them, lightning

flashed and thunder exploded. The rain fell in torrents. I went at a walking pace and was soon obliged to stop because my horse had got stuck and I couldn't see a thing. Somehow or other I found shelter by a large bush. Hunched down and covering up my face, I was waiting patiently for the storm to end, when suddenly by the light of a lightning flash I thought I saw a tall figure on the road. I began looking intently in that direction and saw that the figure had literally sprung from the earth just beside my droshky.

'Who is it?' asked a loud voice.

'Who are you?'

'I'm the local forester.'

I named myself.

'Ah, I know you. On your way home, are you?'

'Yes. But you can see, what a storm . . .'

'Yes, a storm,' the voice responded.

A white lightning flash lit up the forester from head to toe. A crackling thunderclap followed immediately afterwards. The rain beat down with redoubled force.

'It'll not be over soon,' the forester went on.

'What's to be done?'

'Let me lead you to my cottage,' he said sharply.

'Please.'

'Kindly take your seat.'

He went up to the head of the horse, took hold of the bridle and gave a tug. We set off. I clung to the cushion on the droshky which swayed 'like a boat on the waves' and called to my dog. My poor mare splashed about

heavily in the mud, slipping and stumbling, while the forester hovered to right and left in front of the shafts like a
ghost. We travelled for quite a long while until my guide
finally came to a stop.

'Here we are at home, sir,' he said in a calm voice.

The garden gate creaked and several dogs started bark-
ing in unison. I raised my head and saw by the light of a
lightning flash a small cottage set in a large courtyard surrounded by wattle fencing. From one small window a
light shone faintly. The forester led the horse up to the
porch and banged on the door. 'Coming! Coming!' rang
out a thin, small voice, followed by a sound of bare feet
and the squeaky drawing of the bolt, and a little girl of
about twelve, in a shirt tied with selvedge and with a lantern in her hand, appeared on the doorstep.

'Show the gentleman the way,' he said to the little girl.
'Meanwhile I'll put your droshky under cover.'

She glanced at me and went in. I followed her.

The forester's cottage consisted of one room, smoke-
blackened, low and bare, without slats for bedding or par-
titions. A torn sheepskin coat hung on the wall. On a
bench lay a single-barrelled gun and in one corner a pile
of rags; beside the stove stood two large jugs. A taper
burned on the table, sadly flaring up, then guttering. In
the very centre of the cottage hung a cradle tied to the end
of a long pole. The little girl extinguished the lantern,
seated herself on a tiny bench and began with her right
hand to rock the cradle and with her other to adjust the
taper. I looked around me and my heart sank, because it's

not a happy experience to enter a peasant cottage at night. The baby in the cradle breathed heavily and quickly.

'Are you all by yourself here?' I asked the little girl.

'I am,' she said scarcely audibly.

'You're the forester's daughter?'

'Yes,' she whispered.

The door squeaked and the forester came across the threshold, ducking his head. He lifted the lantern off the floor, went to the table and lit the wick.

'It's likely you're not used to just a taper, are you?' he said and shook his curls.

I looked at him. I'd rarely seen such a fine figure of a man. He was tall, broad-shouldered, with a splendid physique. Beneath the damp, coarse cloth of his shirt his powerful muscles stood out clearly. A black curly beard covered half his severe, masculine features and beneath broad eyebrows which met in the middle there gazed out small hazel eyes. He lightly placed his hands on his hips and stood in front of me.

I thanked him and asked him his name.

'I'm called Foma,' he answered, 'but I'm nicknamed Loner.'

'So you're the one called Loner?'

I looked at him with redoubled interest. From my Yermolay and others I'd often heard stories about the Loner whom all the local peasants feared like fire. According to them there wasn't a better master of his job in the world: 'He won't let you take so much as a bit o' brushwood! It doesn't matter when it is, even at dead o' night, he'll be down on you like a ton o' snow, an' you'd best not think of puttin' up a fight—he's as strong and skilful as a devil! An' you can't bribe him, not with drink, not with money, not with any trickery. More'n once there's good folks've tried to drive him off the face of the earth, but he's not given up.'

That's how the local peasants spoke about Loner.

'So you're Loner,' I repeated. 'I've heard about you, my friend. They say you won't let a thing go.'

'I look after my job,' he answered sombrely. 'I'm not eating my master's bread for nothing.'

He took a chopper from his belt, squatted down on the floor and began to hack out a taper.

'You've no lady of the house?' I asked him.

'No,' he answered and struck a heavy blow with the chopper.

'She's dead, is she?'

'No . . . Yes . . . She's dead,' he added and turned away.

I said nothing. He raised his eyes and looked at me.

'She ran off with a passer-by, a fellow from the town,' he pronounced with a cruel smile. The little girl bowed her head. The baby woke up and started crying. The little girl went to the cradle. 'Here, give him this,' said Loner, thrusting a dirty feeding bottle into her hand. 'She even abandoned him,' he went on in a low voice, pointing at the baby. He went to the door, stopped and turned round.

'You'll likely, sir,' he began, 'not want to eat our bread, but apart from bread I've . . .'

'I'm not hungry.'

'Well, you know how it is. I'd light the samovar, only I've got no tea . . . I'll go out and see how your horse is.'

He went out and banged the door. I again looked around. The cottage seemed to me even more miserable than before. The bitter odour of stale woodsmoke made it hard for me to breathe. The little girl didn't move from where she was and didn't raise her eyes. From time to time she gave the cradle a rock and modestly drew her shirt over her shoulders. Her bare feet hung down motionlessly.

'What's your name?' I asked her.

'Ulita,' she said, lowering her sad little face even further.

The forester came in and sat on the bench.

'The storm's passing,' he remarked after a short silence. 'If you say so, I'll lead you out of the forest.'

I rose. Loner picked up his gun and examined the breech-block.

'What's that for?' I asked.

'There's something going on in the forest . . . Someone's felling wood up on Mare's Ridge,' he added, in answer to my questioning look.

'Can you hear it from here?'

'Outside I can.'

We left together. The rain had stopped. In the far distance heavy masses of cloud still crowded together and long streaks of lightning flickered, but above our heads dark–blue patches of sky could be seen here and there and

tiny stars twinkled through sparse, swiftly fleeting clouds.
The outlines of trees, drenched in rain and shaken by the
wind, began to emerge from the darkness. We started listening. The forester took off his cap and bent his head.

'There! . . . There!' he said suddenly and pointed. 'My,
what a night he's chosen for it!'

I didn't hear a thing apart from the noise of leaves.
Loner led the horse out from under the awning.

'It's likely,' he added aloud, 'I'll not get there in time.'

'I'll come with you . . . Is that all right?'

'All right,' he answered and put the horse back. 'We'll
catch him and then I'll lead you out. Let's go.'

We set off, Loner in front and I behind him. God
knows how he knew the way, but he stopped only occasionally and then just to listen to the sound of the axe.

'See,' he hissed through his teeth, 'd'you hear it? D'you
hear it?'

'But where?'

Loner shrugged his shoulders. We descended into a
gully, the wind dropped for a moment and the regular
sounds of an axe clearly reached my hearing. Loner
looked at me and nodded. We went further through wet
bracken and nettles. A muffled and prolonged cracking
sound was heard.

'He's felled it,' said Loner.

Meanwhile the sky continued to clear and in the forest
it became just a bit brighter. Finally we made our way out
of the gully.

'You wait here,' the forester whispered to me, bent

down and, raising his gun aloft, disappeared among the bushes. I began listening intensely. Through the wind's constant noise I thought I heard such faint sounds as an axe carefully cutting off branches, the creaking of wheels and the snorting of a horse.

'Where're you going? Stop!' the iron voice of Loner suddenly cried out.

Another voice cried out plaintively, like a trapped hare. Then a struggle ensued.

'Li-ar! Li-ar!' asserted Loner, breathing hard. 'You'll not get away . . .'

I dashed off in the direction of the noise and, stumbling at each step, ran to the site of the struggle. The forester was busy with something on the ground beside a felled tree: he was holding the thief under him and twisting his arm round his back with a belt. I approached. Loner straightened up and set the other on his feet. I saw a peasant all damp and in tatters, with a long straggly beard. A wretched little horse, half-covered by an awkward piece of matting, also stood there along with the flat cart. The forester didn't say a word, the peasant also. He merely shook his head.

'Let him go,' I whispered in Loner's ear. 'I'll pay for the wood.'

Loner silently seized the horse by its mane with his left hand while with his right he held the thief by his belt.

'Well, get a move on, you good-for-nothing,' he said sternly.

'There's my axe there,' mumbled the thief.

'No point it getting lost!' exclaimed the forester and picked the axe up.

We set off and I followed along behind. The rain started again and soon it began to pour. We made our way with difficulty back to the cottage. Loner abandoned the little horse in the middle of the yard, led the peasant into the room, slackened the knotted belt and set him down in a corner. The little girl, who'd been asleep beside the stove, jumped up and started looking at us in silent fright. I sat down on a bench.

'It's such a downpour,' remarked the forester, 'we'll have to wait a bit. Would you like to lie down?'

'Thank you.'

'I'd lock 'im up in that cupboard, for your sake,' he went on, pointing at the peasant, 'only there's no bolt, as you can see . . .'

'Leave him be, don't touch him,' I broke in.

The peasant glanced at me from under his brows. Inwardly I made myself promise to free the poor wretch no matter what happened. He was sitting motionless on a bench. By the light of the lantern I could make out his haggard, wrinkled face, the jaundiced overhanging brows, restless eyes and thin limbs. The little girl lay down on the floor at his very feet and went to sleep again. Loner sat at the table, leaning his head on his hands. A cricket chirruped in the corner. The rain beat down on the roof and slid down the windows. We were all silent.

'Foma Kuzmich,' the peasant began suddenly in a hollow, broken voice, 'Foma Kuzmich . . .'

'What's up wi' you?'

'Let me go.'

Loner didn't answer.

'Let me go . . . It's bein' hungry . . . Let me go.'

'I know your sort,' the forester said sombrely. 'You're all the same where you come from, a bunch of thieves!'

'Let me go,' repeated the peasant. 'It's the bailiff, you know . . . ruined is what we are . . . Let me go!'

'Ruined! . . . No one's got a right to thieve.'

'Let me go, Foma Kizmich! Don't do me in! Your master, you know yourself, he'll gobble me up, just you see!'

Loner turned away. The peasant shivered as if in a fever. He continuously shook his head and breathed unevenly.

'Let me go,' he repeated in miserable despair, 'for God's sake! I'll pay, just you see, by God I will! By God, it's bein' hungry . . . an' the babes cryin', you know what it's like. It gets real hard, just you see.'

'But you none the less shouldn't go thieving.'

'My little horse,' the peasant went on, 'let 'er go, she's all I got . . . Let 'er go!'

'I'm telling you I can't. I'm also one who takes orders and I'll have to answer for it. And I've got no reason to be kind to the likes of you.'

'Let me go! Need, Foma Kuzmich, need as ever was, that's what . . . Let me go!'

'I know your sort!'

'Just let me go!'

'What's the point of talking to you, eh? You sit there

quietly, otherwise you know what you'll get from me, don't you? Can't you see there's a gentleman here?'

The poor fellow dropped his eyes. Loner yawned and rested his head on the table. The rain still went on. I waited to see what would happen.

The peasant suddenly straightened himself. His eyes were burning and his face had gone red.

'Well, eat me, go on, stuff yourself!' he began, screwing up his eyes and turning down the corners of his mouth. 'Go on, you bloody bastard, suck my Christian blood, go on, suck!'

The forester turned round.

'I'm talkin to you, you bloody Asian, you bloodsucker!'

'Drunk, are you, that's why you've started swearing at me, eh?' said the forester in astonishment. 'Lost your senses, have you?'

'Drunk, ha! Not on your money I wouldn't, you bloody bastard, bloody animal you, animal, animal!'

'Hey, that's enough from you! I'll give you what for!'

'What's it to me! It's all the same—I'll be done for! What can I do without a horse? Kill me—it'll be the same end, if it's from hunger or from you, it's all the same to me! It's all over, wife, children—it's all done for! Just you wait, though, we'll get you in the end!'

Loner stood up.

'Hit me! Hit me!' shouted the peasant in a voice of fury. 'Come on, hit me! Hit me!' (The little girl quickly scrambled up from the floor and stared at him.) 'Hit me! Hit me!'

'Shut up!' thundered the forester and took two steps towards him.

'Enough, Foma, enough!' I cried. 'Leave him be! God be with him!'

'I won't shut up!' the wretch went on. 'It's all the same to me—I'll be done for! You bloody bastard, you animal, you, there's no end to what you do, but just you wait and see, you won't be lordin' it round here much longer! There'll be a tight noose round your neck, just you wait!'

Loner seized him by the shoulder. I hurled myself to the peasant's aid.

'Don't touch him, sir!' the forester shouted at me.

I didn't pay any attention to his threat and was about to stretch out my hand when, to my extreme astonishment, he pulled the belt from the peasant's elbows with one twist, seized him by the nape of the neck, shoved his hat on his head, flung open the door and pushed him out.

'Go to hell with your horse!' he shouted after him. 'Take care you don't come my way again!'

He returned to the cottage and began fussing about in a corner.

'Well, Loner,' I said at last, 'you've astonished me! I realize you're an excellent fellow.'

'Enough of that, sir,' he interrupted me in annoyance. 'Please be good enough not to talk about it. I'd better be leading you out,' he added, ' 'cos you know the rain's not going to wait for you . . .'

The wheels of the peasant's cart rattled away out of the yard.

'Look, he's off!' he said. 'I'll give 'im what for!'

Half an hour later I said goodbye to him at the edge of the forest.

Meeting

I was sitting in a birch wood one autumn, about the middle of September. From early morning there had been occasional drizzle, succeeded from time to time by periods of warm sunny radiance; a season of changeable weather. The sky was either covered with crumbling white clouds or suddenly clear for an instant in a few places, and then, from behind the parted clouds, blue sky would appear, lucid and smiling, like a beautiful eye. I sat and looked around me and listened. The leaves scarcely rustled above my head; by their very noise one could know what time of year it was. It was not the happy, laughing *tremolo* of spring, not the soft murmuration and long-winded talkativeness of summer, not the shy and chill babblings of late autumn, but a hardly audible dreamy chattering. A faint wind ever so slightly moved through the treetops. The interior of the wood, damp from the rain, was continually changing, depending on whether the sun was shining or whether it was covered by cloud; the interior was either flooded with light, just as if everything in it had suddenly smiled: the delicate trunks of the not-too-numerous birches would suddenly acquire the soft sheen of white silk, the wafer-thin leaves which lay on the ground would suddenly grow multi-coloured and burn with crimson and gold, while the beautiful stems of tall curly bracken, already embellished with their autumn colouring which resembles the colour of overripe grapes, would stand there shot through with light, endlessly entangling and crisscrossing before one's eyes; or suddenly one would again be surrounded by a bluish dusk: the bright colours would instantly be extinguished and the birches would all stand there white, without a gleam on them, white as snow that has only just fallen and has not yet been touched by the chilly sparkling rays of the winter sun; and secretively, slyly, thinly drizzling rain would begin to filter and whisper through the wood.

The foliage on the birches was still almost completely green, although it had noticeably faded; only here and there stood a young tree all decked out in red or gold, and one could not help watching how brightly it flared up when the sun's rays broke, gliding and scintillating, through the myriad network of fine branches only just washed by glittering rain. There was not a single bird to be heard: all had taken cover and fallen silent; only the mocking little voice of the tom-tit tinkled occasionally like a little steel bell.

Before I had stopped in this little birch wood, I had gone with my dog through a grove of tall aspens. I confess that I am not particularly fond of that tree—the aspen—with its pale–mauve trunk and grey–green, metallic foliage which it raises as high as possible and spreads out in the air like a quivering fan; nor do I like the continual flutterings of its round untidy leaves which are so awkwardly attached to their long stalks. It acquires beauty only on certain summer evenings when, rising on high in isolation among low bushy undergrowth, it meets the challenge of the ebbing rays of the sunset and gleams and trembles, suffused from its topmost branches to its roots by a uniform yellow and purple light; or when, on a clear windy day, it is all noisily streaming and babbling against the blue sky, and every leaf, seized by the wind's ardour, appears to want to tear itself free, fly away and hurry off into the distance. But in general I dislike this tree and therefore, without stopping to rest in the aspen grove, I made my way to the little birch wood, settled myself under a tree whose branches began close to the ground and were able, in consequence, to shelter me from the rain, and, having gazed admiringly at the surrounding view, fell into the kind of untroubled and mild sleep familiar only to hunters.

I cannot say how long I was asleep, but when I opened my eyes the entire interior of the wood was filled with sunlight and in all directions through the jubilantly rustling foliage a bright blue sky peered and seemed to sparkle; the clouds had vanished, dispersed by the wind that had sprung up; the weather had cleared, and in the air could be felt that special dry freshness which, imbuing the heart with a feeling of elation, almost always means a peaceful and clear evening after a rainy day.

I was on the point of rising and again trying my luck, when suddenly my eyes lighted on a motionless human form. I looked closely and saw that it was a young peasant girl. She was sitting twenty paces from me, her head lowered in thought and both hands dropped on her knees; in the half-open palm of one of them lay a thick bunch of wild flowers and at each breath she took the bunch slipped quietly down on to her checked skirt. A clean white blouse, buttoned at the neck and at the wrists, gathered in short soft folds about her waist; two rows of large yellow beads fell from her neck on to her bosom. She was very pretty in her own way. Her thick fair hair of a beautiful ash colour was parted into two carefully styled semicircles below a narrow crimson ribbon drawn almost down to her temples, which were white as ivory; the rest of her face was faintly sunburned to that golden hue which is only acquired by a delicate skin. I could not see her eyes because she did not raise them; but I clearly saw her fine, high eyebrows and long eyelashes, which were damp, and on one of her cheeks I saw the dried trace of a tear that had come to rest at the edge of her slightly pale lips and glittered in the sunlight. The whole appearance of her head was very charming; even the slightly thick and rounded nose did nothing to spoil it. I particularly liked the expression on her face for the way in which it was so artless and gentle, so melancholy and full of childish bewilderment at her own grief.

She was evidently waiting for someone. Something crackled faintly in the wood and she at once raised her head and looked round; in the transparent shade her large eyes, bright and frightened, flashed quickly before me like the eyes of a doe. She listened for a few moments without taking her wide-open eyes from the place where the faint sound had been made, then heaved a sigh, turned her head calmly back, bent still farther down and began slowly to finger the flowers. Her eyelids reddened, her lips gave a quiver of bitterness and another tear slipped from beneath her thick lashes, coming to rest on her cheek where it glittered radiantly. Some time passed in this way, and the poor girl did not move save to make a few regretful gestures with her hands and to go on listening and listening. Again something made a noise in the wood and she was instantly alerted. The noise continued, grew louder as it approached, and finally could be heard the noise of rapid, decisive footsteps. She straightened herself and appeared to be overcome with shyness; her attentive features began to quiver and burn with expectation. The figure of a man could be glimpsed through the thicket. She peered in that direction, blushed suddenly, gave a joyful and happy smile, got ready to stand up and once again suddenly lowered her head, growing pale and confused— and she only raised her faltering, almost imploring gaze to the newcomer when he had stopped beside her.

I examined him with curiosity from my hiding-place. I confess that he produced an unpleasant impression on me. To all appearances he was the pampered valet of some rich young master. His clothes displayed pretensions to good taste and dandified casualness: they consisted of a short, bronze-coloured top-coat buttoned up to the neck and inherited, more than likely, from his master, a little rose-tinted neck-tie with mauve tips and a black velvet cap with gold lace edging worn pulled down over the eyebrows. The rounded collar of his white shirt pressed unmercifully up against his ears and bit into his cheek, while his starched cuffs covered his hands right down to the red and crooked fingers which were embellished with gold and silver rings containing turquoise forget-me-nots. His face—ruddy, fresh-complexioned and impudent—belonged to the category of faces which, so far as I have been able to judge, almost invariably annoy men and, unfortunately, are very often pleasing to women. He clearly made an effort to endow his rather coarse features with an expression of superciliousness and boredom; he endlessly screwed up his already tiny milk–grey eyes, frowned, let his mouth droop at the edges, gave forced yawns and with a casual, though not entirely skilled, air of abandon either patted the reddish, artfully coiled hair on his temples or twiddled the little yellow hairs that stuck out on his fat upper lip—in a word, he showed off insufferably. He began to show off as soon as he saw the young peasant girl waiting for him; he slowly approached her at a lounging pace, came to a stop, shrugged his shoulders, stuck both hands into the pockets of his top-coat and, with hardly more than a fleeting and indifferent glance at the poor girl, lowered himself to the ground.

'Well,' he began, still looking away to one side, swinging his leg and yawning, 'have you been here long?'

The girl was unable to answer him immediately.

'A long time, sir, Victor Alexandrych,' she said eventually in a scarcely audible voice.

'Ah!' He removed his cap, grandly drew his hand through his thick, tightly coiled hair, which began almost at his eyebrows, and glancing round with dignity, once more carefully covered his priceless head. 'And I'd almost completely forgotten. After all, look how it rained!' He yawned once more. 'There's a mass of things to be done, what with everything to be got ready and the master swearing as well. Tomorrow we'll be off . . .'

'Tomorrow?' the girl said and directed him a look of fright.

'That's right—tomorrow. Now, now, now, please,' he added hastily and with annoyance, seeing that she had begun to tremble all over and was quietly lowering her head, 'please, Akulina, no crying. You know I can't stand crying.' And he puckered up his snub nose. 'If you start, I'll leave at once. What silliness—blubbering!'

'No, I won't, I won't,' Akulina uttered hurriedly, making herself swallow her tears. 'So you're leaving tomorrow?' she added after a brief pause. 'When will God bring you back to see me again, Victor Alexandrych?'

'We'll meet again, we'll meet again. If not next year, then later. It seems the master wants to enter government service in St Petersburg,' he continued, speaking the words casually and slightly through the nose, 'and maybe we'll go abroad.'

'You'll forget me, Victor Alexandrych,' Akulina said sadly.

'No, why should I? I won't forget you. Only you've got to be sensible, not start playing up, obey your father . . .

I'll not forget you—no-o-o.' And he calmly stretched himself and again yawned.

'You mustn't forget me, Victor Alexandrych,' she continued in an imploring voice. 'I've loved you so much, it seems, and it seems I've done everything for you ... You tell me to listen to my father, Victor Alexandrych ... There's no point in listening to my father ...'

'Why not?' He uttered these words as it were from his stomach, lying on his back with his arms behind his head.

'There's no point, Victor Alexandrych. You know that yourself ...'

She said nothing. Victor played with the steel chain of his watch.

'You're not a fool, Akulina,' he started saying at last, 'so don't talk nonsense. I want what's best for you, do you understand me? Of course, you're not stupid, you're not a complete peasant girl, so to speak; and your mother also wasn't always a peasant girl. But you're without any education, so you've got to listen when people tell you things.'

'I'm frightened, Victor Alexandrych.'

'Hey, there, that's a lot of nonsense, my dear. What's there to be frightened of! What's that you've got there,' he added, turning to her, 'flowers?'

'Flowers,' answered Akulina despondently. 'They're some field tansies I've picked,' she continued, brightening slightly, 'and they're good for calves. And these are marigolds, they help against scrofula. Just look what a lovely little flower it is! I've never seen such a lovely little flower before in all my born days. Then there are some forget-me-nots, here are some violets. But these I got for you,' she added, taking out from beneath the yellow tansies a small bunch of blue cornflowers tied together with a fine skein of grass, 'would you like them?'

Victor languidly stretched out his hand, took the bunch, casually sniffed the flowers and began to twiddle them in his fingers, gazing up in the air from time to time with thoughtful self-importance. Akulina looked at him and her sad gaze contained such tender devotion, such worshipful humility and love. Yet she was also afraid of him, and fearful of crying; and taking her own leave of him and doting on him for the last time; but he lay there in the lounging pose of a sultan and endured her worship of him with magnanimous patience and condescension. I confess that his red face vexed me with its pretentiously disdainful indifference through which could be discerned a replete and self-satisfied vanity. Akulina was so fine at that moment, for her whole heart was trustfully and passionately laid open before him, craving him and yearning to be loved, but he . . . he simply let the cornflowers drop on the grass, took a round glass in a bronze frame out of the side pocket of his top-coat and started trying to fix it in place over his eye; but no matter how hard he tried to keep it in place with a puckered brow, a raised cheek and even with his nose, the little eyeglass kept on falling out and dropping into his hand.

'What's that?' Akulina asked finally in astonishment.

'A lorgnette,' he answered self-importantly.

'What's it for?'

'So as to see better.'

'Show it me.'

Victor frowned, but he gave her the eyeglass.

'Don't break it, mind.'

'You needn't worry, I won't.' She raised it timidly to her eye. 'I don't see anything,' she said artlessly.

'It's your eye, you've got to screw up your eye,' he retorted in the voice of a dissatisfied mentor. She screwed up the eye before which she was holding the little glass. 'Not that one, not that one, idiot! The other one!' exclaimed Victor and, giving her no chance to correct her mistake, took the lorgnette from her.

Akulina reddened, gave a nervous laugh and turned away.

'It's obviously not for the likes of me,' she murmured.

'That's for sure!'

The poor girl was silent and let fall a deep sigh.

'Oh, Victor Alexandrych, what'll I do without you?' she suddenly said.

Victor wiped the lorgnette with the edge of his coat and put it back in his pocket.

'Yes, yes,' he said eventually, 'it sure will be hard for you to start with.' He gave her several condescending pats on the shoulder; she ever so quietly lifted his hand from her shoulder and timidly kissed it. 'Well, all right, all right, you're a good kid,' he went on, giving a self-satisfied smile, 'but what can I do about it? Judge for yourself! The master and I can't stay here; it'll be winter soon now and to spend the winter in the country—you know this yourself—is just horrible. But it's another matter in St Petersburg! There are simply such wonderful things there, such as you, stupid, wouldn't be able to imagine even in your wildest dreams! What houses and streets, and the society, the culture—it's simply stupendous!' Akulina listened to him with greedy interest, her lips slightly parted like a child's. 'Anyhow,' he added, turning over, 'why am I telling you all this? You won't be able to understand it.'

'Why say that, Victor Alexandrych? I've understood it, I've understood everything.'

'What a bright one you are!'

Akulina lowered her head.

'You never used to talk to me like that before, Victor Alexandrych,' she said without raising her eyes.

"Didn't I before? Before! You're a one! Before indeed!" he commented, pretending to be indignant.

Both were silent for a while.

'However, it's time for me to be going,' said Victor, and was on the point of raising himself on one elbow.

'Stay a bit longer,' Akulina declared in an imploring voice.

'What's there to wait for? I've already said goodbye to you.'

'Stay a bit,' Akulina repeated.

Victor again lay back and started whistling. Akulina never took her eyes off him. I could tell that she was slowly working herself into a state of agitation: her lips were working and her pale cheeks were faintly crimsoning.

'Victor Alexandrych,' she said at last in a breaking voice, 'it's sinful of you ... sinful of you, Victor Alexandrych, in God's name it is!'

'What's sinful?' he asked, knitting his brows, and he raised himself slightly and turned his head towards her.

'It's sinful, Victor Alexandrych. If you'd only say one kind word to me now you're leaving, just say one word to me, wretched little orphan that I am ...'

'But what should I say to you?'

'I don't know. You should know that better than me, Victor Alexandrych. Now you're going away, and if only you'd say a word ... Why should I deserve this?'

'What a strange girl you are! What can I say?'

'Just say one word ...'

'Well, you've certainly gone on and on about the same thing,' he said in disgruntlement and stood up.

'Don't be angry, Victor Alexandrych,' she added quickly, hardly restraining her tears.

'I'm not angry, it's only that you're stupid ... What do you want? You know I can't marry you, don't you? Surely you know I can't? So what's it you want? What is it?' He stuck his face forward in expectation of her answer and opened wide his fingers.

'I don't want anything ... anything," she answered, stammering and scarcely daring to stretch her trembling hands out towards him, 'only if you'd just say one word in farewell ...'

And tears streamed from her eyes.

'Well, so there it is, you've started crying,' Victor said callously, tipping his cap forward over his eyes.

'I don't want anything,' she went on, swallowing her tears and covering her face with both hands, 'but what'll it be like for me in the family, what'll there be for me? And what's going to happen to me, what's going to become of me, wretch that I am! They'll give their orphan girl away to someone who doesn't love her . . . O poor me, poor me!'

'Moan away, moan away!' muttered Victor under his breath, shifting from one foot to the other.

'If only he'd say one little word, just one word . . . Such as, Akulína, I . . . I . . .'

Suddenly heart-rending sobs prevented her from finishing what she was saying. She flopped on her face in the grass and burst into bitter, bitter tears. Her whole body shook convulsively, the nape of her neck rising and falling. Her long-restrained grief finally poured forth in torrents. Victor stood for a moment or so above her, shrugged his shoulders, turned and walked away with big strides.

Several moments passed. She grew quiet, raised her head, jumped up, looked about her and wrung her hands; she was on the point of rushing after him, but her legs collapsed under her and she fell on her knees. I could not hold myself back and rushed towards her, but she had hardly had time to look at me before she found the strength from somewhere to raise herself with a faint cry and vanish through the trees, leaving her flowers scattered on the ground.

I stopped there a moment, picked up the bunch of cornflowers and walked out of the wood into a field. The sun was low in the pale clear sky and its rays had, as it were, lost their colour and grown cold; they did not shine so much as flow out in an even, almost watery, light. No more than half an hour remained until evening, but the sunset was only just beginning to crimson the sky. A flurrying wind raced towards me across the dry, yellow stubble; hastily spinning before it, little shrivelled leaves streamed past me across the track and along the edge of the wood; the side which faced on to the field like a wall shuddered all over and glistened with a faint sparkling, distinctly though not brightly; on the red-tinted grass, on separate blades of grass, on pieces of straw, everywhere innumerable strands of autumn cobwebs glittered and rippled. I stopped, and a feeling of melancholy stole over me, for it seemed to me that the sombre terror associated with the approaching winter was breaking through the cheerless, though fresh, smile of nature at this time of withering. High above me, ponderously and sharply sundering the air with its wings, a vigilant raven flew by, turned its head, looked sidewards at me, took wing and disappeared beyond the wood with strident cawings; a large flock of pigeons rose smartly from a place where there had been threshing and after suddenly making a huge wheeling turn in the air settled busily on to the field—a sure sign of autumn! Someone rode by on the other side of a bare hillock, his empty cart clattering noisily . . .

I returned home; but the image of the poor Akulina took a long time to fade from my mind, and her cornflowers, which have long since withered, remain with me to this day . . .

Living Relic

Homeland of longsuffering—
Thou art the land of Russia!
—F. Tyutchev

There is a French saying which runs: 'A dry fisherman and a wet hunter have the same sad look.' Never having had a fondness for catching fish, I am unable to judge what a fisherman must experience at a time of fine, clear weather and to what extent, when the weather is bad, the pleasure afforded him by an excellent catch outweighs the unpleasantness of being wet. But for a hunter rainy weather is a veritable calamity. It was precisely to such a calamity that Yermolay and I were subjected during one of our expeditions after grouse in Belev county. The rain did not let up from dawn onwards. The things we did to be free of it! We almost covered our heads completely with our rubber capes and took to standing under trees in order to catch fewer drips—yet the waterproof capes, not to mention the way they interfered with our shooting, let the water through in a quite shameless fashion; and as for standing under trees—true, at first it did seem that there were no drips, but a little later the moisture which had gathered in the foliage suddenly broke its way through

31

and every branch doused us with water as if it were a rainpipe, cold dribbles gathered under my collar and ran down the small of my back ... That was the last straw, as Yermolay was fond of saying.

'No, Pyotr Petrovich,' he exclaimed eventually, 'we can't go on with this! We can't hunt today. All the scent's being washed out for the dogs and the guns are misfiring ... Phew! What a life!'

'What do we do, then?' I asked.

'This is what. We'll drive to Alekseyevka. Perhaps you don't know it, but there's a small farm of that name belonging to your mother, about five miles away. We can spend the night there, and then tomorrow ...'

'We'll come back here?'

'No, not here ... I know some places on the other side of Alekseyevka. They're a lot better than this for grouse!'

I refrained from asking my trusty companion why he had not taken me straightaway to those places, and that very same day we reached the farm belonging to my mother, the very existence of which, I admit, I had not suspected until that moment. The farmhouse had an adjacent cottage of considerable antiquity, but not lived-in and therefore clean; here I spent a reasonably quiet night.

The next day I awoke pretty early. The sun had only just risen and the sky was cloudless. All around glistened with a strong, two-fold brilliance: the brilliance of the youthful rays of morning light and of yesterday's downpour. While a little cart was being got ready for me, I set off to wander a little way through the small, once fruit-bearing but now wild, orchard, which pressed up on all sides against the cottage with its richly scented, luxuriantly fresh undergrowth. Oh, how delightful it was to be in the open air, under a clear sky in which larks fluttered, whence poured the silver beads of their resonant song! On their wings they probably carried drops of dew, and their singing seemed to be dew-sprinkled in its sweetness. I even removed my cap from my head and breathed in joyfully, lungfuls at a time . . . On the side of a shallow ravine, close by the wattle fencing, a bee-garden could be seen; a small path led to it, winding like a snake between thick walls of weeds and nettles, above which projected— God knows where they had come from—sharp-tipped stalks of dark-green hemp.

I set off this path and reached the bee-garden. Next to it there stood a little wattle shed, a so-called *amshanik*, where the hives are put in winter. I glanced in through the half-open door: it was dark, silent and dry inside, smelling of mint and melissa. In a corner boards had been fixed up and on them, covered by a quilt, a small figure was lying. I turned to go out at once.

'Master, but master! Pyotr Petrovich!' I heard a voice say, as faintly, slowly and hoarsely as the rustling of marsh sedge.

I stopped.

'Pyotr Petrovich! Please come here!' the voice repeated. It came to me from the corner, from those very boards which I had noticed.

I drew close and froze in astonishment. In front of me

there lay a live human being, but what kind of human being was it?

The head was completely withered, of a uniform shade of bronze, exactly resembling the colour of an ancient icon painting; the nose was as thin as a knife-blade; the lips had almost disappeared—only the teeth and eyes gave any gleam of light, and from beneath the kerchief wispy clusters of yellow hair protruded on to the temples. At the chin, where the quilt was folded back, two tiny hands of the same bronze colour slowly moved their fingers up and down like little sticks. I looked more closely and I noticed that not only was the face far from ugly, it was even endowed with beauty, but it seemed awesome none the less and incredible. And the face seemed all the more awesome to me because I could see that a smile was striving to appear on it, to cross its metallic cheeks—was striving and yet could not spread.

'Master, don't you recognize me?' the voice whispered again: it was just like condensation rising from the scarcely quivering lips. 'But how would you recognize me here! I'm Lukeria ... Remember how I used to lead the dancing at your mother's, at Spasskoye ... and how I used to be the leader of the chorus, remember?'

'Lukeria!' I cried. 'Is it you? Is it possible?'

'It's me, master—yes, it's me, Lukeria.'

I had no notion what to say, and in a state of shock I gazed at this dark, still face with its bright, seemingly lifeless eyes fixed upon me. Was it possible? This mummy was Lukeria, the greatest beauty among all the maid servants in our house, tall, buxom, white-skinned and rosy-cheeked, who used to laugh and sing and dance! Lukeria, talented Lukeria, who was sought after by all our young men, after whom I myself used to sigh in secret, I—a sixteen-year-old boy!

'Forgive me, Lukeria,' I said at last, 'but what's happened to you?'

'Such a calamity overtook me! Don't feel squeamish, master, don't turn your back on my misfortune—sit down on that little barrel, bring it closer, so as you'll be able to hear me ... See how talkative I've become! ... Well, it's glad I am I've seen you! How ever did you come to be in Alekseyevka?'

Lukeria spoke very quietly and faintly, but without pausing.

'Yermolay the hunter brought me here. But go on with what you were saying ...'

'About my misfortune, is it? If that's what you wish, master. It happened to me long, long ago, six or seven years ago. I'd just then been engaged to Vasily Polyakov—remember him, such a fine upstanding man he was, with curly hair, and in service as wine butler at your mother's house. But by that time you weren't here in the country any longer—you'd gone off to Moscow for your schooling. We were very much in love, Vasily and I. I couldn't get him out of my mind; it all happened in the springtime. One night—it wasn't long to go till dawn—I couldn't sleep, and there was a nightingale singing in the garden so wonderfully sweetly! I couldn't bear it, and I got up and

35

went out on to the porch to listen to it. He was pouring out his song, pouring it out . . . and suddenly I imagined I could hear someone calling me in Vasya's voice, all quiet like: "Loosha! . . ." I glanced away to one side and, you know, not awake properly, I slipped right off the porch step and flew down—bang!—on to the ground. And, likely, I hadn't hurt myself so bad, because—soon I was up and back in my own room. Only it was just like something inside—in my stomach—had broken . . . Let me get my breath back . . . Just a moment, master.'

Lukeria fell silent, and I gazed at her with astonishment. What amazed me was the almost gay manner in which she was telling her story, without groans or sighs, never for a moment complaining or inviting sympathy.

'Ever since that happened,' Lukeria continued, 'I began to wither and sicken, and a blackness came over me, and it grew difficult for me to walk, and then I even began to lose control of my legs—I couldn't stand or sit, I only wanted to lie down all the time. And I didn't feel like eating or drinking: I just got worse and worse. Your mother, out of the goodness of her heart, had medical people to look at me and sent me to hospital. But no relief for me came of it all. And not a single one of the medicals could even say what kind of an illness it was I had. The things they didn't do to me, burying my spine with red-hot irons and sitting me in a chopped-up ice—and all for nothing. In the end I got completely stiff . . . So the masters decided there was no good in trying to cure me any more, and because there wasn't room for a cripple in their house

36

. . . well, they sent me here—because I have relations here. So here I'm living, as you see.'

Lukeria again fell silent and again endeavoured to smile.

'But this is horrible, this condition you're in!' I exclaimed, and not knowing what to add, I asked: 'What about Vasily Polyakov?' It was a very stupid question.

Lukeria turned her eyes a little to one side.

'About Polyakov? He grieved, he grieved—and then he married someone else, a girl from Glinnoye. Do you know Glinnoye? It's not far from us. She was called Agrafena. He loved me very much, but he was a young man—he couldn't be expected to remain a bachelor all his life. And what sort of a companion could I be to him? He's found himself a good wife, who's a kind woman, and they've got children now. He's steward on the estate of one of the neighbours: your mother released him with a passport, and things are going very well for him, praise be to God.'

'And you can't do anything except lie here?' I again inquired.

'This is the seventh year, master, that I've been lying like this. When it's summer I lie here, in this wattle hut, and when it begins to get cold—then they move me into a room next to the bath-house. So I lie there, too.'

'Who comes to see you? Who looks after you?'

'There are kind people here as well. They don't leave me by myself. But I don't need much looking after. So far as feeding goes, I don't eat anything, and I have water—there it is in that mug: it always stands by me full of pure spring water. I can stretch out to the mug myself, because I've still got the use of one arm. Then there's a little girl here, an orphan; now and then she drops by, and I'm grateful to her. She's just this minute gone ... Did you meet her? She's so pretty, so fair-skinned. She brings me flowers—I'm a great one for them, flowers, I mean. We haven't any garden flowers. There used to be some here, but they've all disappeared. But field flowers are pretty too, and they have more scent than the garden flowers. Lilies-of-the-valley now—there's nothing lovelier!'

'Aren't you bored, my poor Lukeria, don't you feel frightened?'

'What's a person to do? I don't want to pretend—at first, yes, I felt very low, but afterwards I grew used to it, I learnt to be patient—now it's nothing. Others are much worse off.'

'How do you mean?'

'Some haven't even got a home! And others are blind or dumb! I can see perfectly, praise be to God, and I can hear everything, every little thing. If there's a mole digging underground, I can hear it. And I can smell every scent, it doesn't matter how faint it is! If the buckwheat is just beginning to flower in the field or a lime tree is just blossoming in the garden, I don't have to be told: I'm the first to smell the scent, if the wind's coming from that direction. No, why should I make God angry with my complaints? Many are worse off than I am. Look at it this way: a healthy person can sin very easily, but my sin has gone out of me. Not long ago Father Aleksey, the priest, was beginning to give me communion and he said: "There can't be any need to hear your confession, for how can you sin in your condition?" But I answered him: "What about a sin of the mind, father?" "Well," he said and laughed, "that kind of sin's not very serious."

'And, it's true, I'm not really sinful even with sins of the mind,' Lukeria went on, 'because I've learned myself not to think and, what's more, not even to remember. Time passes quicker that way.'

This surprised me, I must admit.

'You are so much by yourself, Lukeria, so how can you prevent thoughts from entering your head? Or do you sleep all the time?'

'Oh, no, master! Sleep's not always easy for me. I may not have big pains, but something's always gnawing at me, right there inside me, and in my bones as well. It doesn't let me sleep as I should. No . . . I just lie like this and go on lying here, not thinking. I sense that I'm alive, I breathe—and that's all there is of me. I look and I smell scents. Bees in the apiary hum and buzz, then a dove comes and sits on the roof and starts cooing, and a little brood-hen brings her chick in to peck crumbs; then a sparrow'll fly in or a butterfly—I enjoy it all very much. The year before last swallows made a nest over there in the corner and brought up their young. Oh, how interesting that was! One of them would fly in, alight on the little nest, feed the young ones—and then off again. I'd take another look and there'd be another swallow there in place of the first. Sometimes it wouldn't fly in but just go

39

past the open door, and then the baby birds'd start chirping and opening their little beaks ... The next year I waited for them, but they say a hunter in these parts shot them with his gun. Now what good could he have got from doing that? After all, a swallow's no more harm than a beetle. What wicked men you are, you hunters!'

'I don't shoot swallows,' I hastened to point out.

'And one time,' Lukeria started to say again, 'there was a real laugh! A hare ran in here! Yes, really! Whether dogs were chasing him or not, I don't know, only he came running straight in through the door! He sat down quite close and spent a long time sniffing the air and twitching his whiskers—a regular little officer he was! And he took a look at me and realized that I couldn't do him any harm. Eventually he upped and jumped to the door and looked all round him on the doorstep—he was a one, he was! Such a comic!'

Lukeria glanced up at me, as if to say: wasn't that amusing? To please her, I gave a laugh. She bit her dried-up lips.

'In the winter, of course, things are worse for me. I'm left in the dark, you see—it's a pity to light a candle and anyhow what'd be the good of it? I know how to read and was always real keen on reading, but what's there to read here? There are no books here, and even if there were, how would I be able to hold it, the book, I mean? Father Aleksey brought me a church calendar so as to distract me, but he saw it wasn't any use and picked it up and took it away again. But even though it's dark, I've always got something to listen to—maybe a cricket'll start chirruping or a mouse'll begin scratching somewhere. That's when it's good not to be thinking at all!'

After a short rest, Lukeria continued: 'Or else I say prayers. Only I don't know many of them, of those prayers. And why should I start boring the Lord God with my prayers? What can I ask him for? He knows better than I do what's good for me. He sent me a cross to carry, which means he loves me. That's how we're ordained to understand our suffering. I say Our Father, and the prayer to the Blessed Virgin, and I sing hymns for all who sorrow—and then I lie still without a single thought in my mind. Life's no bother to me!'

Two minutes went by. I did not break the silence and I did not stir on the narrow barrel which served as a place for me to sit. The cruel, stony immobility of the unfortunate living being who lay before me affected me also, and I became literally rigid.

'Listen, Lukeria,' I began finally. 'Listen to what I want to propose to you. Would you like it if I arranged for you to be taken to a hospital, a good town hospital? Who knows, but maybe they can still cure you? At least you won't be by yourself . . .'

Lukeria raised her brows ever so slightly.

'Oh, no, master,' she said in an agitated whisper, 'don't send me to a hospital, let me alone. I'll only have to endure more agony there. There's no good in trying to cure me! Once a doctor came here and wanted to have a look at me. I said to him, begging him: "Don't disturb me for Christ's sake!" What good was it! He started turning me this way and that, straightening and bending my legs and arms and telling me: "I'm doing this for learning, that's why. I'm one who serves, a scientist! And don't you try to stop me, because they've pinned a medal on me for my contributions to science and it's for you, you dolts, that I'm working so hard." He pulled me about and pulled me about, named what was wrong with me—and a fine name it was!—and with that he left. But for a whole week afterwards my poor bones were aching. You say I'm alone, all the time by myself. No, not all the time. People come to see me. I'm quiet and I'm not a nuisance to anyone. The peasant girls come sometimes for a chat. Or a holy woman will call in on her wanderings and start telling me about Jerusalem and Kiev and the holy cities. I'm not frightened of being by myself. Truly it's better, truly it is! Let me alone, master, don't move me to hospital. Thank you, you're a good man, only leave me alone, my dear.'

'Just as you wish, as you wish, Lukeria. I was only suggesting it for your own good . . .'

'I know, master, it was for my own good. But, master, my dear one, who is there that can help another person? Who can enter into another's soul? People must help themselves! You won't believe it, but sometimes I lie by myself like I am now—and it's just as if there was no one on the whole earth except me. And I'm the only living person! And a wondrous feeling comes over me, as if I'd been visited by some thought that seizes hold of me—something wonderful it is.'

'What do you think about at such times, Lukeria?'

'It's quite impossible to say, master—you can't make it out. And afterwards I forget. It comes out like a cloud and pours its rain through me, making everything so fresh and good, but what the thought was really you can never understand! Only it seems to me that if there were people round me—none of that would have happened and I'd never feel anything except my own misfortune.'

Lukeria sighed with difficulty. Like the other parts of her body, her breast would not obey her wishes.

'As I look at you now, master,' she began again, 'you feel very sorry for me. But don't you pity me too much, don't you do that! See, I'll tell you something: sometimes even now I . . . You remember, don't you, what a gay one I was in my time? One of the girls! . . . D'you know something? I sing songs even now.'

'Songs? You really sing?'

'Yes, I sing songs, the old songs, roundelays, feast songs, holy songs, all kinds! I used to know many of them, after all, and I haven't forgotten them. Only I don't sing the dancing songs. In my present state that wouldn't be right.'

'How do you sing them—to yourself?'

'To myself and out loud. I can't sing them loudly, but they can still be understood. I was telling you that a little girl comes to visit me. An orphan, that's what she is, but she understands. So I've been teaching her and she's picked up four songs already. Don't you believe me? Wait a moment, I'll show you . . .'

Lukeria drew upon all her reserves of energy. The idea that this half-dead being was preparing to sing aroused in me a spontaneous feeling of horror. But before I could utter a word, a long-drawn, scarcely audible, though clear sound, pitched on the right note, began to quiver in my ears, followed by another, then a third. Lukeria was singing 'I walked in the meadows of green grieving for my life'. She sang without altering the expression on her petrified face, even gazing fixedly with her eyes. But so touchingly did this poor, forced, wavering little voice of hers resound, rising like a wisp of smoke, that I ceased to feel horror: an indescribable piteousness compressed my heart.

'Oh, I can't any more!' she uttered suddenly. 'I've no strength left . . . I've rejoiced so very much already at seeing you.'

She closed her eyes.

I placed my hands on her tiny cold fingers. She looked up at me and her dark eyelids, furred with golden lashes like the lids of ancient statuary, closed again. An instant later they began to glisten in the semi-darkness. Tears moistened them.

As before, I did not stir.

'Silly of me!' Lukeria uttered suddenly with unexpected strength and, opening her eyes wide, attempted to blink away the tears. 'Shouldn't I be ashamed? What's wrong with me? This hasn't happened to me for a long time—

44

not since the day Vasya Polyakov visited me last spring. While he was sitting with me and talking it was all right. But when he'd gone—how I cried then all by myself! Where could so many tears come from! For sure a woman's tears cost nothing. Master,' Lukeria added, 'if you have a handkerchief, don't be finicky, wipe my eyes.'

I hastened to do what she asked, and left the handkerchief with her. She tried to refuse at first, as if she were asking why she should be given such a present. The handkerchief was very simple, but clean and white. Afterwards she seized it in her feeble fingers and did not open them again. Having grown accustomed to the darkness which surrounded us both, I could clearly distinguish her features and could even discern the delicate flush which rose through the bronze of her face and could make out in her face—or so at least it seemed to me—traces of her past beauty.

'Just now you were asking me, master,' Lukeria started saying again, 'whether I sleep. I certainly don't sleep often, but every time I have dreams—wonderful dreams! I never dream that I'm ill. In my dreams I'm always so young and healthy . . . I've only one complaint: when I wake up, I want to have a good stretch and yet here I am, just as if I were bound in fetters. Once I had such a marvellous dream! Would you like me to tell it to you? Well, listen, I dreamt of myself standing in a field, and all around me there was rye, so tall and ripe, like gold . . . And there was a little rust-red dog with me, wickedly vicious it was, all the time trying to bite me. And I had a sickle in my hand, and it wasn't a simple sickle, but it was the moon when the moon has the shape of a sickle. And with the moon itself I had to reap the rye until it was all cut. Only I grew very tired from the heat, and the moon blinded me, and a languor settled on me; and all around me cornflowers were growing—such big ones! And they all turned their little heads towards me. And I thought I would pick these cornflowers, because Vasya had promised to come, so I'd make myself a garland first of all and then still have time to do the reaping. I began to pluck the cornflowers, but they started to melt away through my fingers, to melt and melt, no matter what I did! And I couldn't weave myself a garland. And then I heard someone coming towards me, coming close up to me and calling: "Loosha! Loosha!" Oh dear, I thought, I'm too late! It doesn't matter, though, I thought, because I can put the moon on my head instead of the cornflowers. So I put the moon on my head, and it was just like putting on one of those tall bonnets—at once I glowed with light from head to foot and lit up all the field around me. I looked, and there, through the very tips of the heads of rye, someone was smoothly approaching ever so quickly—only it wasn't Vasya, it was Christ Himself! And why I knew it was Christ I can't say—He's never depicted as I saw Him—but it was Him! He was beardless, tall, young, clad all in white, except for a belt of gold, and He put out a hand to me and said: "Fear not, for thou art My chosen bride, come with Me. In My heavenly kingdom thou shalt lead

46

the singing and play the songs of paradise." And how firmly I pressed my lips to His hand. Then my little dog seized me by the legs, but at once we ascended up into the heavens, He leading me, and His wings stretched out to fill the heavens, as long as the wings of a gull—and I followed after Him! And the little dog had to leave go of me. It was only then that I understood that the little dog was my affliction and that there was no place for my affliction in the Kingdom of Heaven.'

Lukeria fell silent for a minute.

'But I also had another dream,' she began again, 'or perhaps it was a vision I had—I don't know which. It seemed that I was lying in this very wattle hut and my dead parents—my mother and my father—came to me and bowed low to me, but without saying anything. And I asked them: "Why do you, my mother and father, bow down to me?" And they answered and said: "Because thou hast suffered so greatly in this world, thou hast lightened not only thine own soul but hast also lifted a great weight from ours. And for us in our world the way has been made easier. Thou hast already done with thine own sins and art now conquering ours." And, having said this, my parents again bowed low to me—and then I couldn't see them any longer: all I could see were the walls. Afterwards I was very full of doubt whether such a thing had happened to me. I told the priest of it, only he said it couldn't have been a vision, because visions are vouchsafed only to those of ecclesiastical rank.

'Then there was yet another dream I had,' Lukeria con-

tinued. 'I saw myself sitting beside a big road under a willow, holding a whittled stick, with a bag over my shoulders and my head wrapped in a kerchief, just like a holy
wanderer! And I had to go somewhere far, far away on a
pilgrimage, offering prayers to God. And the holy wan-
derers, the pilgrims, were continually going past me; they
were walking quietly past me, as if unwillingly, all the
time going in the same direction; and their faces were all
sad and very much alike. And I saw that weaving and hur-
rying among them was one woman, a whole head taller
than all the others, and she wore a special kind of dress,
not our kind, not like a Russian dress. And her face was
also of a special kind, stern and severe, like the face of
one used to fasting. And it seemed that all the others
made way for her; and then she suddenly turned and
came straight towards me. She stopped and looked at me.
Her eyes were like the eyes of a falcon, yellow and big
and bright as could be. And I asked her: "Who are you?"
And she said to me: "I am your death." I should've been
frightened, but instead I was happy as a child, I swear to
God I was! And this woman, my death, said to me: "I am
sorry for you, Lukeria, but I cannot take you with me.
Farewell!" O Lord, what sorrow there was for me then!
"Take me," I cried, "beloved mother, dear one, take
me!" And my death turned to face me and began to
speak . . . And I understood that she was appointing the
hour when I should die, but I couldn't quite grasp it, it
wasn't clear, except that it would be some time after Saint

48

Peter's Day . . . Then I woke up. Such surprising dreams I've been having!'

Lukeria raised her eyes to the ceiling and grew reflective.

'Only I have this one trouble, that a whole week may pass and I never once go to sleep. Last year there was a lady who came by, saw me and gave me a little bottle with some medicine to make me sleep. She told me to take ten drops each time. That was a great help to me, and I slept. Only now that little bottle's long ago finished. Do you know what that medicine was and how to get it?'

The lady who came by obviously gave Lukeria opium. I promised to procure such a little bottle for her and again could not restrain myself from remarking aloud at her patience.

'Oh, master!' she protested. 'What d'you mean by that? What sort of patience? Now Simon Stilites' patience was really great: he spent thirty years on a pillar! And there was another of God's servants who ordered himself to be buried in the ground up to his chest, and the ants ate his face . . . And here's something else that an avid reader of the Bible told me: there was a certain country, and that country was conquered by the Hagarenes, and they tortured and killed all who lived therein; and no matter what those who lived there did, they could in no way free themselves. And there appeared those who dwelt in that country a holy virgin; she took a mighty sword and arrayed herself in heavy amour and went out against the Hagarenes and did drive them all across the sea. But when she

49

had driven them away, she said to them: "Now it is time that you should burn me, for such was my promise, that I should suffer a fiery death for my people." And the Hagarenes seized her and burned her, but from that time forward her people were freed for ever! Now that's a really great feat of suffering! Mine's not like that!'

I wondered to myself in astonishment at the distance the legend of Joan of Arc had travelled and the form it had taken, and after a brief silence I asked Lukeria how old she was.

'Twenty-eight . . . or twenty-nine. I'm not thirty yet. What's the good o counting them, the years, I mean! I'll tell you something else . . .'

Lukeria suddenly coughed huskily and gave a groan.

'You are talking a great deal,' I remarked to her, 'and it could be bad for you.'

'That's true,' she whispered, hardly audible. 'Our little talk's got to end, no matter what happens! Now that you'll be going I'll be quiet as long as I wish. I've unburdened my heart to the full . . .'

I began to take leave of her, repeating my promise to send her the medicine and imploring her again to give careful thought to my question whether there was anything that she needed.

'I don't need anything, I'm quite content, praise God,' she uttered with the greatest of effort, but moved by my concern. 'God grant everyone good health! And you, master, tell your mother that, because the peasants here are poor, she should take a little less in rent from them! They haven't enough land, there isn't an abundance of anything . . . They'd give thanks to God for you if you did that . . . But I don't need a thing—I'm quite content.'

I gave Lukeria my word that I would fulfil her request and was already on the way to the door when she called to me again.

'Remember, master,' she said, and something wondrous glimmered in her eyes and on her lips, 'what long tresses I had? Remember, they reached right down to my knees! For a long time I couldn't make up my mind . . . Such long hair! . . . But how could I comb it out? In my state, after all! . . . So I cut it all off . . . Yes, that's what I did . . . Well, master, forgive me! I can't go on any more . . .'

That very day, before setting out for the hunt, I had a talk about Lukeria with the farm overseer. I learned from him that she was known in the village as the 'Living Relic' and that, in this regard, there had never been any trouble from her; never a murmur was to be heard from her, never a word of complaint. 'She herself asks for nothing, but, quite to the contrary, is thankful for everything; a quiet one, if ever there was a quiet one, that's for sure. Struck down by God, most likely for her sins,' the overseer concluded, 'but we don't go into that. And as, for instance, for passing judgment on her—no, we don't pass judgement. Let her alone!'

A few weeks later I learned that Lukeria had died. Her death had come for her, as she thought—'after Saint Peter's Day.' There were rumours that on the day of her death she heard a bell ringing all the time, although from Alekseyevka to the church is a matter of three miles or more and it was not a Sunday. Lukeria, however, said that the ringing did not come from the church, but 'from above'. Probably she did not dare to say that it came from heaven.

APOLLONIUS OF RHODES · *Jason and the Argonauts*
ARISTOPHANES · *Lysistrata*
SAINT AUGUSTINE · *Confessions of a Sinner*
JANE AUSTEN · *The History of England*
HONORÉ DE BALZAC · *The Atheist's Mass*
BASHŌ · *Haiku*
AMBROSE BIERCE · *An Occurrence at Owl Creek Bridge*
JAMES BOSWELL · *Meeting Dr Johnson*
CHARLOTTE BRONTË · *Mina Laury*
CAO XUEQIN · *The Dream of the Red Chamber*
THOMAS CARLYLE · *On Great Men*
BALDESAR CASTIGLIONE · *Etiquette for Renaissance Gentlemen*
CERVANTES · *The Jealous Extremaduran*
KATE CHOPIN · *The Kiss and Other Stories*
JOSEPH CONRAD · *The Secret Sharer*
DANTE · *The First Three Circles of Hell*
CHARLES DARWIN · *The Galapagos Islands*
THOMAS DE QUINCEY · *The Pleasures and Pains of Opium*
DANIEL DEFOE · *A Visitation of the Plague*
BERNAL DÍAZ · *The Betrayal of Montezuma*
FYODOR DOSTOYEVSKY · *The Gentle Spirit*
FREDERICK DOUGLASS · *The Education of Frederick Douglass*
GEORGE ELIOT · *The Lifted Veil*
GUSTAVE FLAUBERT · *A Simple Heart*
BENJAMIN FRANKLIN · *The Means and Manner of Obtaining Virtue*
EDWARD GIBBON · *Reflections on the Fall of Rome*
CHARLOTTE PERKINS GILMAN · *The Yellow Wallpaper*
GOETHE · *Letters from Italy*
HOMER · *The Rage of Achilles*
HOMER · *The Voyages of Odysseus*